Little Blossom Stories

Gramps Has a Dog

By Cecilia Minden

Sport is a farm dog.

Sport likes to bark at the farm cats.

4

Sport sees a big cat with black
and white fur.

Sport barks at the big cat with black and white fur.

Oh, no! That is not a black and white cat.

That is a black and white skunk!

8 The skunk sprays Sport.

The spray smells bad.

Sport needs a good scrub in a big tub.

Gramps gives Sport a good scrub
in a big tub.

12 Now, Sport does not smell bad.

Now, Sport smells good.

Word List

sight words

a	likes	Oh
and	needs	sees
does	no	the
good	Now	The

short vowel words

at	cats
bad	farm
bark	in
barks	is
big	not
cat	tub

blends and digraphs

black	spray
Gramps	sprays
scrub	That
skunk	white
smell	with
Sport	

Sport is a farm dog.

Sport likes to bark at the farm cats.

Sport sees a big cat with black and white fur.

Sport barks at the big cat with black and white fur.

Oh, no! That is not a black and white cat.

That is a black and white skunk!

The skunk sprays Sport.

The spray smells bad.

Sport needs a good scrub in a big tub.

Gramps gives Sport a good scrub in a big tub.

Now, Sport does not smell bad.

Now, Sport smells good.

Published in the United States of America by Cherry Lake Publishing Group
Ann Arbor, Michigan
www.cherrylakepublishing.com

Illustrator: Becky Down

Cherry Blossom Press is an imprint of Cherry Lake Publishing Group.

Library of Congress Cataloging-in-Publication Data

Names: Minden, Cecilia, author. | Down, Becky, illustrator.
Title: Gramps has a dog / by Cecilia Minden ; illustrated by Becky Down.
Description: Ann Arbor, Michigan : Cherry Lake Publishing, 2021. | Series:
  Little blossom stories
Identifiers: LCCN 2021007826 (print) | LCCN 2021007827 (ebook) | ISBN
  9781534187986 (paperback) | ISBN 9781534189386 (pdf) | ISBN
  9781534190788 (ebook)
Subjects: LCSI I. Readers (Primary)
Classification: LCC PE1119.2 .M56374 2021 (print) | LCC PE1119.2 (ebook)
  | DDC 428.6/2–dc23
LC record available at https://lccn.loc.gov/2021007826
LC ebook record available at https://lccn.loc.gov/2021007827

Cecilia Minden is the former director of the Language and Literacy Program at Harvard Graduate School of Education. She earned her PhD in Reading Education at the University of Virginia. Dr. Minden has written extensively for early readers. She is passionate about matching children to the very book they need to improve their skills and progress to a deeper understanding of all the wonder books can hold. Dr. Minden and her family live in McKinney, Texas. Dr. Minden would like to thank her great-niece, Grace Keough, for her help in writing these books. Grace is a seven-year-old with dreams of being a writer. She is constantly putting together books. The illustrations included!

CHERRY BLOSSOM PRESS